Samuel French Acting Edition

Kiss

by Guillermo Calderón

MUSIC USE NOTE

Licensees are solely responsible for obtaining formal written permission from copyright owners to use copyrighted music in the performance of this play and are strongly cautioned to do so. If no such permission is obtained by the licensee, then the licensee must use only original music that the licensee owns and controls. Licensees are solely responsible and liable for all music clearances and shall indemnify the copyright owners of the play(s) and their licensing agent, Samuel French, against any costs, expenses, losses and liabilities arising from the use of music by licensees. Please contact the appropriate music licensing authority in your territory for the rights to any incidental music.

IMPORTANT BILLING AND CREDIT REQUIREMENTS

If you have obtained performance rights to this title, please refer to your licensing agreement for important billing and credit requirements.

Arabic translation of the dialogue by Nathalie Khankan.
Arabic translation of "Yama Mweil El-Hawa" by Hassan Awwad.

KISS was first produced at Schauspiel Düsseldorf in Germany in 2014. The production was directed by Guillermo Calderón, with set and costume design by Anna Sophia Röpcke, dramaturgy by Almut Wagner, and lighting design by Konstantin Sonneson. The cast was as follows:

HADEEL / ANDREA . . . . .Simin Soraya

YOUSSIF / DANIEL . . . . Marian Kindermann

AHMED / MARTIN . . . . .Gregor Löbel

BANA / LAURA . . . . .Anna Kubin

WOMAN / AMEERA'S SISTER . . . . .Nadin Jaroubi

INTERPRETER. . . . . Katharina Leufen / Linda Marek

CHARACTERS

HADEEL / ANDREA

YOUSSIF / DANIEL

AHMED / MARTIN

BANA / LAURA

WOMAN / AMEERA'S SISTER

INTERPRETER

(The living room and kitchen of an apartment. Two doors: one to the hallway of the apartment building, one to a bathroom upstage. Table, chairs. Two big sofas.)

(A projection on the wall reads: Damascus 2014.)

*(**HADEEL** walks in from the bathroom and turns on the TV.)*

(Someone knocks on the door.)

*(**HADEEL** opens the door. It's **YOUSSIF**.)*

HADEEL. Oh...

YOUSSIF. Hello.

HADEEL. Hello.

YOUSSIF. Hello.

HADEEL. Sit down.

YOUSSIF. Thank you... And the others?

HADEEL. They're not here yet.

(Pause.)

YOUSSIF. Oh... What time is it?

HADEEL. There's plenty of time.

YOUSSIF. Yes... I know. I came here a little bit early.

HADEEL. Yeah.

(Pause.)

Good. Did you see yesterday's episode?

YOUSSIF. Yes I did. Of course. You?

HADEEL. Of course. Yes. Super.

YOUSSIF. Yes. It was.

HADEEL. Yes.

YOUSSIF. *(Making fun of the actors on TV.)* Do you see this knife?

HADEEL. *I do.*

YOUSSIF. *Do you know whose blood it is?*

HADEEL. *Yes. I know.*

YOUSSIF. I love that stuff.

HADEEL. Yes. *Give up. Give up. Give. Up.*

YOUSSIF. *Yes.*

HADEEL. *Give up. The police will find you anyway. The police? Me? Impossible. Who is going to tell them? You?*

YOUSSIF. *Yes. I am going to tell them. Me. And you will end up in prison, like a dirty rat.*

HADEEL. *No... No. Don't tell them. Forgive me. Please forgive me. Forgive me and I can give you my family's money. I can become your wife.*

YOUSSIF. My wife?

(*Pause.*)

HADEEL. Wife. Yes...

YOUSSIF. That's very good.

HADEEL. I know. Isn't it?

(*Pause.*)

YOUSSIF. Yes. Nobody's here yet?

HADEEL. No. Why?

YOUSSIF. Nothing. It's just that... We're never alone.

HADEEL. No. We're never alone.

YOUSSIF. Where is Ahmed?

HADEEL. I don't know.

YOUSSIF. But is he coming?

HADEEL. Yes. He is. Of course.

YOUSSIF. But he's not in here?

HADEEL. No. Right now he's not. No.

YOUSSIF. OK.

(*Pause.*)

HADEEL. What's wrong with you?

YOUSSIF. Me?

HADEEL. Yes. You.

YOUSSIF. Nothing…

HADEEL. What?

YOUSSIF. Nothing.

HADEEL. What is it?

(Silence.)

I know what's wrong. "Nothing." Ahhhh. What the fuck is wrong with you? Why are you here so fucking early?

YOUSSIF. Sorry. I just came to watch the soap opera.

HADEEL. Just came here to watch the soap opera…

YOUSSIF. Yes.

HADEEL. I know. But it's too fucking early. I'm not going to be able to cook. The tea is not ready. Why don't you just fucking leave and never come back again?

(Silence.)

YOUSSIF. Hadeel.

HADEEL. What?

YOUSSIF. I can't go.

HADEEL. Why?

YOUSSIF. I can't.

HADEEL. Why?

YOUSSIF. Because…we're all getting together tonight. Here. And last night I was thinking a lot about you.

HADEEL. Please…

YOUSSIF. I was thinking about you and I thought… I thought, Hadeel needs a house. She needs a bed. She needs food. She needs her French books…

HADEEL. Youssif…

YOUSSIF. Wait… And I thought, maybe she doesn't need me. No. But I do. I need her. I do. I do. And I don't need a house, I don't need food, I don't need the books I've never read. No. But I need her. I need you. I need to touch your sweater. I need to smell you. I need you and I don't care if you don't need me. Just tell Ahmed…

HADEEL. Ahmed?

YOUSSIF. Yes.

HADEEL. Ahmed is my boyfriend.

YOUSSIF. I know.

HADEEL. And your best friend.

YOUSSIF. Yes.

HADEEL. Ahmed is my boyfriend.

YOUSSIF. I know.

HADEEL. What?

YOUSSIF. He's your boyfriend.

HADEEL. Good. And you know why Ahmed is my boyfriend?

YOUSSIF. No.

HADEEL. No you don't. You don't know why. Ahmed is my boyfriend because I love him. And he loves me back. And that makes me love him even more, and that bigger love makes him love me back again even more. So whenever he says he loves me I say I love you back. It's magic. Is that too hard to understand?

YOUSSIF. Hadeel.

HADEEL. Answer.

YOUSSIF. Hadeel, what's all this shit about love?

HADEEL. It's love. You don't know what love is? What are you talking about?

YOUSSIF. Of course I do. Everyone loves everyone. I don't care. Even I love everyone. Everyone. People in the street, my people. I love them all. I want to give them a hug. But I don't want to hug them, to touch them, as much as I want to touch you.

> *(Pause.)*

HADEEL. Shut up, Youssif. You have a girlfriend.

YOUSSIF. I know.

HADEEL. And she's coming here tonight.

YOUSSIF. I know.

HADEEL. Shut up.

(*Pause.*)

Did you talk to her about this?

YOUSSIF. Not yet... But I will. I just I want to be part of you, Hadeel. And I know that you love Ahmed...but let me tell you... It is totally human to love two men at the same time.

HADEEL. What?

YOUSSIF. Try to love the two of us.

HADEEL. No... No. No. That's disgusting.

YOUSSIF. No it's not.

HADEEL. Yes it is. It is.

YOUSSIF. No, it's not. You know what I'm talking about. You can love two men at the same time. You can. The heart is a big muscle and yours is bigger than normal. I know. And it happens to a lot of women. They are in love with one man and then one day they meet another man and they don't know why but they hate him. Why? Because they secretly like him. And that is the beginning of a second love. They feel it's treason. But they can't stop. They can't. They love two different men. And then naturally there will be broken hearts, screams, tears, even blood, the same old story. But, Hadeel...

Listen...even if you love him you have every right to choose the man who really makes you happy. Not the one who promises you a wonderful future but the one who shows you happiness here and now. And that man is me. You know that. I've seen it in your eyes. Right now you can despise me. You can even hate me. But that's just the beginning of something... You have two loves right now. I know it. Choose me, Hadeel... Choose me. Forgive me for being so honest. I just want you to be my wife.

HADEEL. Youssif...

YOUSSIF. What?

HADEEL. Please.

YOUSSIF. Be my wife.

HADEEL. I can't move.

YOUSSIF. I'm sorry. I understand. I've been watching you. I've seen how you talk to Bana. You worship her. You try on her shoes. You comb her hair. You laugh at her handwriting. You cry when you watch her acting in her soap operas. She's a wonderful actress. And you love her. And you don't want to hurt her.

HADEEL. Youssif...

YOUSSIF. What?

HADEEL. What about Bana!

YOUSSIF. We'll lose her.

HADEEL. I can't.

YOUSSIF. But we'll have each other.

HADEEL. I can't.

YOUSSIF. Please, Hadeel. I love you.

HADEEL. Youssif...stop. Stop... Please. I...

YOUSSIF. What?

HADEEL. I despise you, Youssif, you pretentious fuck. All this talk about smell...and you smell like a fucking horse. But...I'm no better. No. I've made so many mistakes. I'm weak. Weak. Every time I have a problem I just read and eat vanilla ice cream. And now... Now I have the perfect boyfriend. Ahmed is perfect for me. Perfect. He is. He makes me laugh. But...you. You. I'm so dirty, Youssif. I'm so...dirty. And you are so...you disgust me. But...I do want to go home with you. I can't believe this... Every time you and Bana come here to watch TV...when you leave I just want to scream TAKE ME, Youssif. TAKE ME WITH YOU. I just want to kiss your leather jacket. I want to put you to sleep. Forgive me, Bana. Youssif. I want to see you naked. I want to see you eat and when you are done I want to lick your plate until it's completely clean.

YOUSSIF. Please marry me.

HADEEL. No...

YOUSSIF. Hadeel.

HADEEL. Don't touch me.

YOUSSIF. Marry me.

HADEEL. Leave me alone.

YOUSSIF. Hadeel…

HADEEL. Yes…

YOUSSIF. Yes?

HADEEL. Yes.

YOUSSIF. Yes, what?

HADEEL. Yes, Youssif. I will marry you. I will.

YOUSSIF. Hadeel.

HADEEL. Don't touch me. Not now. If we start now we won't be able to stop.

>*(Knocking at the door.)*

YOUSSIF. Bana or Ahmed.

HADEEL. If it's Ahmed I'll talk to him.

YOUSSIF. OK.

HADEEL. I'll need time. Open the door. I love you.

YOUSSIF. I love you too.

>*(**HADEEL** goes to the bathroom. **YOUSSIF** opens the door, steps into the hallway to talk with **AHMED**.)*

AHMED. Hello.

YOUSSIF. Hi.

>*(They hug.)*

AHMED. How are you?

YOUSSIF. Good. Nervous.

AHMED. I know. Me too.

YOUSSIF. The soap opera.

AHMED. Yeah…the soap opera. Of course.

YOUSSIF. Of course, listen…do you have cigarettes? I don't have any.

AHMED. Yeah. I do.

YOUSSIF. How many?

AHMED. A new pack.

YOUSSIF. Great. But I need a fresh pack for myself. I will go and get some.

AHMED. Wait.

YOUSSIF. Why?

AHMED. Where is she?

YOUSSIF. What? In the bathroom.

AHMED. OK.

YOUSSIF. OK. Bye.

AHMED. No. Wait.

YOUSSIF. What?

AHMED. Stay one second.

YOUSSIF. Ahmed...

AHMED. Look. Listen...

YOUSSIF. Yes?

AHMED. Good...

(*Pause.*)

YOUSSIF. What's wrong?

AHMED. Nothing. Listen... I'm going to marry her.

YOUSSIF. Who?

AHMED. Hadeel.

YOUSSIF. Hadeel?

AHMED. Of course.

YOUSSIF. Great. Congratulations.

AHMED. Thank you. I'm fucking nervous.

YOUSSIF. Sure...sure. Congratulations.

AHMED. Thank you.

YOUSSIF. When did you propose to her?

AHMED. Not yet. I'm going to ask her now.

YOUSSIF. Now?

AHMED. Yes.

YOUSSIF. Oh. But we were going to watch TV.

AHMED. I know, I was going to propose before the soap opera but you beat me, / you were faster than me.

YOUSSIF. Yeah. I was faster than you.

AHMED. Yes. Go get your cigarettes.

YOUSSIF. Yes. Yes. Sure. I'll leave you two alone... Listen. Ahmed... Congratulations. But don't do it right now.

AHMED. Why?

YOUSSIF. It's not really romantic.

AHMED. I know. I don't care. I'm not romantic.

YOUSSIF. Yes. I understand. I love you. Just be brave. And strong.

AHMED. Yeah.

YOUSSIF. Be a man. I love you. Always.

AHMED. Thank you.

> *(They hug.)*

YOUSSIF. You're shaking.

AHMED. I know. Look.

> *(His hand shakes.)*

YOUSSIF. Look... Maybe you should take a walk first.

AHMED. You think so?

YOUSSIF. Yes. Breathe a little.

AHMED. Right. OK.

YOUSSIF. Go and get me the pack.

> *(He gives **AHMED** money.)*

AHMED. Sure. Good idea.

> *(He takes the money and leaves.)*

YOUSSIF. Go.

AHMED. Thanks.

> *(**YOUSSIF** goes back inside.)*

HADEEL. What's going on?

YOUSSIF. Ahmed.

> *(Pause.)*

HADEEL. Where is he?

YOUSSIF. He left.

HADEEL. *(Coughing.)* He left?

YOUSSIF. Yes. But he'll be right back.

HADEEL. What did you tell him?

YOUSSIF. Nothing. He's buying cigarettes.

HADEEL. Youssif...

YOUSSIF. No. Look...you need to talk to him.

HADEEL. Not now.

YOUSSIF. It has to be now.

HADEEL. Can't we just watch TV? I can talk to him tomorrow.

YOUSSIF. He's going to propose.

HADEEL. What?

YOUSSIF. He just told me. He's going to propose.

HADEEL. No... Why?

YOUSSIF. Because he's in love with you.

HADEEL. No...

YOUSSIF. He's doing it right now.

HADEEL. No. This is...no.

YOUSSIF. It's my fault. Please forgive me.

HADEEL. Wait.

YOUSSIF. Forgive me.

HADEEL. Wait. It's OK.

YOUSSIF. I shouldn't have talked to you today.

HADEEL. I told you it's fine.

YOUSSIF. Please don't tell him anything.

HADEEL. But I have to, Youssif. If he asks me to marry him I can't say yes.

YOUSSIF. Then talk to him tomorrow.

HADEEL. I can't. I will not be able to survive like this, with this secret inside me. Youssif, you don't understand. Every time I hug him I close my eyes and just think about you. When I sleep with him I dream about you and I wake up...happy. I cook for him thinking I'm cooking for you, and when he eats and says he likes the food I just want to scream: *This is not your food. I don't love you anymore. I'm in love with Youssif.*

(Pause.)

YOUSSIF. Let me touch you.

HADEEL. Not yet.

YOUSSIF. Please.

HADEEL. You know I want to but not now.

YOUSSIF. He's coming back in a moment.

HADEEL. I know. How can I do it? I have to break his heart, Youssif.

YOUSSIF. Just be a woman.

HADEEL. Just be a woman... OK. I love you. I'm crazy in love with you.

YOUSSIF. I love you too...and I really want to...

(Knocking on the door.)

(They kiss. **HADEEL** *pushes him away. She opens the door.)*

AHMED. Hello.

HADEEL. Hello.

AHMED. Here you are.

(They hug.)

HADEEL. I was going to cook something.

AHMED. That's great. Thank you.

HADEEL. It's nothing.

YOUSSIF. And the cigarettes?

AHMED. Oh. The cigarettes. I'm sorry... I didn't go. Here's your money.

YOUSSIF. What happened?

AHMED. I just walked around...

HADEEL. Did you see Bana?

AHMED. No. She's still at work?

YOUSSIF. I don't think so.

AHMED. It's late.

YOUSSIF. I know.

HADEEL. She should be here by now.

AHMED. I can go out and look if she's...

HADEEL. No.

YOUSSIF. No... Don't worry. Let me do this. She's my girlfriend.

AHMED. Sure.

YOUSSIF. Bye. Good luck.

AHMED & HADEEL. Thank you.

HADEEL. Bye.

YOUSSIF. Bye.

(He leaves.)

AHMED. How are you?

HADEEL. Great. You?

AHMED. Great. What's wrong with him?

HADEEL. I don't know...

(Pause.)

AHMED. Listen... Hadeel, we need to talk.

HADEEL. Yes.

AHMED. Yes.

HADEEL. We do.

AHMED. Yes... You saw that... I've been walking around the block trying to breathe...like this...because I need to... relax.

HADEEL. What's wrong?

AHMED. Don't worry. I don't want to break up with you.

HADEEL. OK.

AHMED. Good... I just wanted to say... Wait. Why do we need to talk?

HADEEL. You said it.

AHMED. Yes, but you also said we needed to talk.

HADEEL. Yes. Yes...I did.

AHMED. About what?

HADEEL. Nothing...

AHMED. What do you want to talk about?

(Silence.)

I'm waiting.

HADEEL. You go first.

AHMED. No. You.

(Pause.)

HADEEL. OK. I feel... It's hard to explain but... You know... We have known each other since we were five. You know what's going on.

AHMED. No. I don't. What?

HADEEL. Will you do me a favor?

AHMED. Of course.

HADEEL. I'm afraid... I just want to hear your voice. You always soothe me when you talk.

AHMED. Hadeel...

HADEEL. Please... Just talk first. Take a leap.

AHMED. OK. OK. I don't know what's going on but... Listen... Just two things. One, I love you with all my heart. That's one. And two, I want to live my life with you. You make me happy; that's three things, actually.

HADEEL. But Ahmed, you know that sometimes I make you sad.

AHMED. Yes. But that's just because life is not perfect. We are not perfect. We fail...we can be disgusting. I know I am sometimes. But I want to live with you. I want to have...problems with you. I don't know... I don't know, I like your body. I just want to have you. I want to give you everything I have. My blood. I want to give you my life. You are my life... I don't know, Hadeel. Will you marry me?

HADEEL. Ahmed... This is a surprise.

AHMED. I know.

HADEEL. But I can't...

AHMED. What?

HADEEL. I'm... I love you.

AHMED. I love you too, Hadeel.

HADEEL. I do.

AHMED. So?

HADEEL. So yes. I will marry you. Yes. Of course I will. Of course, Ahmed, my love. Thank you. I'm so incredibly happy.

AHMED. Hadeel...

(*Knocking on the door.*)

(**AHMED** *opens.* **YOUSSIF** *enters.*)

And Bana?

YOUSSIF. She hasn't arrived yet.

AHMED. Did you call her?

YOUSSIF. Her phone was off the whole time.

AHMED. Yes.

YOUSSIF. (*To* **AHMED.**) Please forgive me.

AHMED. Yes. Of course.

(*Pause.*)

For what?

YOUSSIF. I'm so sorry. I decided to come back.

AHMED. Oh, don't worry. We had plenty of time to talk.

YOUSSIF. OK.

HADEEL. Yes.

YOUSSIF. So you talked?

AHMED. Yes.

YOUSSIF. Good.

AHMED. We're getting married.

YOUSSIF. Yes?

AHMED. Yes.

YOUSSIF. What?

AHMED. We're getting married. I just proposed.

YOUSSIF. Good. (*To* **HADEEL.**) And what did you say?

HADEEL. I said yes.

AHMED. Don't act so surprised. You knew.

YOUSSIF. Yes. I did. I knew.

HADEEL. You knew?

YOUSSIF. Yes.

AHMED. Yes. I told him when I got here.

HADEEL. Oh.

YOUSSIF. Yes... Congratulations. Congratulations. You're going to be so happy.

HADEEL. Yes. But we are happy right now.

AHMED. We are.

YOUSSIF. Yes. You are. It's true... Please forgive me if I'm not jumping up and down but this is getting to me. You two... Oh... I love the two of you so much...so much... there are so many emotions... It's hard to explain... Let's hug.

(They all hug.)

I too would like to marry the woman I love.

AHMED. Then why don't you do it?

YOUSSIF. I want to.

AHMED. Then do it.

YOUSSIF. Yes...

HADEEL. Youssif...

YOUSSIF. Yes. I should propose tonight. Wouldn't that be great? Two proposals on the same night.

AHMED. It would be wonderful.

YOUSSIF. I love her so much. I'm going to propose tonight. And I'll tell her... Bana, I want to see you naked. I want to see you eat and when you are done I want to lick your plate until it's completely clean.

AHMED. That's great.

HADEEL. She should be here. Where is she?

YOUSSIF. I don't know. Still working.

AHMED. I don't think so.

HADEEL. It's too late.

YOUSSIF. It's very late.

HADEEL. Maybe you shouldn't propose tonight.

YOUSSIF. Why?

AHMED. Why, Hadeel?

(*Knocking on the door.*)

(**HADEEL** *opens.* **BANA** *enters.*)

BANA. Hi.

ALL. Hi.

HADEEL. Where were you?

(*Pause.*)

BANA. Is it on?

AHMED. Not yet.

BANA. Good. Excuse me.

YOUSSIF. Bana...

(**BANA** *goes to the bathroom. They wait.*)

AHMED. What's going on?

YOUSSIF. I don't know.

HADEEL. I think I know.

AHMED. What do you know?

YOUSSIF. What?

HADEEL. Wait.

AHMED. What?

HADEEL. Should we knock?

(**BANA** *returns.*)

YOUSSIF. Are you OK?

(*Pause.*)

What's wrong?

BANA. What's wrong? I kissed someone.

YOUSSIF. What?

BANA. I kissed someone. A kiss.

YOUSSIF. Bana...

BANA. What do you care so much? What do you care about me? You weren't so upset when you were dumping me last night. You said that you were going away forever to work. That you were leaving me to work in Dubai. Yes. But now I think that's just a big, big lie. You lied to my face. You prepared me a cup of tea and you talked all nice and then you hit me with the news that you have to travel? Forever? Go away? Forever? You're not going anywhere. I know. You're staying here. Because there's another woman. I know it. But don't worry. I know you're leaving me but I won't die without you. I won't. But after all these years together I had hoped... Everyone knows that there's a right way to break up, Youssif. If you want to break someone's heart, first you have to become distant and weird so one knows something is wrong and only then, after a few months of that you can stab the knife. The knife called truth. I cheated on you. I don't love you anymore. That's how you do it. But you can't wake me up in the middle of the night and tell me that you want to leave me because you got a job forever in Dubai. It's heartless. And cruel. And I can't believe that's the real reason you are killing me, because until yesterday I was sure you were in love with me. I saw it in your eyes. Which means that I, that I don't know what love is anymore. I'm broken. You damaged me forever. But it's not only my bleeding heart that hurts, it's also my eyes. Now I'm blind. Now I can't see love and beauty.

YOUSSIF. Did you kiss someone?

BANA. I did.

YOUSSIF. How?

HADEEL. Youssif...

AHMED. *(To* **YOUSSIF.***)* Please don't do this...

BANA. My body hurts. My legs. Breathing hurts. I would love to just go to the hospital. Walk in, lay down and say... Undress me. Talk to me. Feed me. Inject me. Give me that plastic bag with the tiny drops. Let me have more blue pills. The red pills. The white. The red and white. The little green ones. The red. Let me press the button. Let me ask for morphine. Let me watch my soap opera. I'm in it. I can tell you how it ends. They get married. Take me to the hospital because I'm hollow inside. My organs are gone. My brain is a cauliflower. Why? Because I just saw the true face of simple men.

HADEEL. You should have stayed at home.

BANA. Yes.

AHMED. Why did you come here?

BANA. I don't know.

HADEEL. Bana... Sit. I can't see you suffer like this. You... You are broken, but look... We are friends. Youssif...he may not love you anymore... I know he's afraid. And I'm sure he did not want to see you suffer. I don't either. You are my sister. You are the only one that can use my toothbrush. You know that.

BANA. Yes.

HADEEL. Yes... But Youssif...you have to understand...you have to know.

BANA. What?

YOUSSIF. Hadeel...

HADEEL. This is not right.

BANA. It's not.

YOUSSIF. Hadeel...

AHMED. What?

HADEEL. Listen... Ahmed, sit. Listen. Youssif said that he loved me.

BANA. What?

YOUSSIF. Hadeel, please.

HADEEL. It's true.

AHMED. Hadeel...

BANA. I'm sorry. I didn't hear right.

HADEEL. It happens every day, Bana. He fell in love with me.

AHMED. What?

BANA. Wait. Did you fall in love with him?

HADEEL. No. No. Of course not. Never. He's just a friend. The lover of my best friend.

BANA. But you seduced him.

HADEEL. No, Bana.

BANA. Yes...you did.

AHMED. Bana, please.

HADEEL. No. I promise you. I did not seduce him. Never. He just fell for me. It happens every day.

BANA. Did he tell you that?

HADEEL. What?

BANA. That he loves you.

HADEEL. Yes.

BANA. When?

HADEEL. Today.

AHMED. Today?

HADEEL. Yes.

AHMED. When?

BANA. How?

HADEEL. Does it matter?

AHMED. Of course it matters.

BANA. It matters to me.

HADEEL. Today. He came in earlier and said that he loves me.

BANA. No.

AHMED. Right before I came in?

YOUSSIF. Yes.

AHMED. But Hadeel...

YOUSSIF. Bana...

BANA. Shut up. *(To* **HADEEL.***)* And what did you say?

HADEEL. Nothing.

YOUSSIF. Hadeel...

BANA. Shut up. Hadeel, you said something. You had to say something. Don't lie to me, Hadeel. Don't lie to me, please. Don't. I've used your toothbrush, Hadeel.

HADEEL. OK. Wait. Wait... Yes. Of course I said something. I did say something.

BANA. What?

HADEEL. I said. Shut your fucking mouth. Shut up. You don't love me. Now you are going to go back to Bana and you're going to tell her that you love her. And if you don't love her anymore you are going to tell her: Bana, I don't love you anymore. OK Youssif, I'm giving you two days to tell her about this. If you don't I'm telling her myself. But if you do tell Bana that you don't love her anymore, please don't tell her that you fell in love with me. Ever. We are going to keep this conversation as a secret forever. Forever.

BANA. Youssif… Why didn't you tell me the truth last night?

YOUSSIF. I was going to tell you but I was afraid… And today you were away all day. I called you but your phone was off. I even went outside to wait for you… I wanted to be honest, but now that doesn't matter because somebody kissed you.

BANA. But why did you have to wait so long to say, I don't love you anymore? You could have told me before. In the summer. When I was washing your white shirt. You could have told me when I was cleaning the blood from your knee with alcohol after you smashed your bicycle into an orange tree. You were smoking, Youssif. And crying. You could have told me when I told you I didn't want to have kids because I love being an actress. Or when you told me that when I was naked I looked just like my mother. Or when you asked me if I would be OK with you sleeping with other women. But you didn't. You didn't. Instead you chose to tell my best friend, my sister, that you love her.

YOUSSIF. Everything is broken. This is total destruction. I can't even think.

HADEEL. Bana, all this will pass. Don't fall. This is not the end of the world. I want to see you smile.

BANA. How?

HADEEL. Let me give you some good news.

BANA. No. Please.

HADEEL. I'm going to get married.

BANA. What?

HADEEL. Yes. Ahmed asked me.

BANA. Well. Congratulations… *(To* **AHMED.***)* When did you propose?

AHMED. Just now.

BANA. In front of Youssif?

AHMED. No. He was outside waiting for you.

BANA. So he had already told Hadeel that he loves her.

AHMED. Yes. And he was happy for me. You were happy for me. At least you looked happy, but Hadeel had just rejected you. You were crying inside. Look at you now. Poor Youssif. I'm sorry but I can't… I really don't wan't to see you suffer like this.

BANA. Hadeel… Congratulations. My sister…

HADEEL. Thank you, Bana.

AHMED. *(To* **HADEEL.***)* Wait. Stop that.

HADEEL. Why? This is completely…

AHMED. This is all wrong.

HADEEL. No.

BANA. Don't be like that right now.

AHMED. *(To* **HADEEL.***)* Why didn't you tell me?

HADEEL. I was going to keep it a secret.

AHMED. Forever?

HADEEL. Yes…

AHMED. But…

HADEEL. People make mistakes.

AHMED. Yes, but this, what happened here changes everything.

HADEEL. It doesn't.

AHMED. Hadeel, don't you see? In the happiest day of my life my dear brother tells my girlfriend that he loves her, and when a few minutes later I tell him that I am going to propose to you he congratulates me. And then my future wife, you, tells me that she is willing to be my wife, while deep inside you're hiding the most horrible secret. Will this be the happiest day of our lives? What did you expect, Hadeel? Were you going to hide this secret from me all your life? And from Bana, your friend, your sister? Don't you know that a sinful secret creates a bond that's...it can be even stronger and deeper than love? Is that what you were thinking about, were those your doubts, the reasons for your surprised look before you said yes?

HADEEL. I did not doubt.

AHMED. Yes. You did doubt. You didn't want to say yes.

HADEEL. No.

BANA. Please, Ahmed. Don't do this. Don't. She loves you with all her heart and you know it. She's your future wife and she's the most honest woman in the world and that's why you still love her. And maybe that's the reason Youssif says he loves her. Because he doesn't have an ounce of honesty in his body.

YOUSSIF. Bana, please.

BANA. Did you congratulate him?

(No answer.)

Youssif...I'm talking to you. Did you congratulate him when he told you he was going to propose to Hadeel?

YOUSSIF. Yes. I had to.

AHMED. I'll never trust anybody again.

YOUSSIF. You don't understand. I told Hadeel I love her. That much is true. And I'm terribly, terribly sorry. But I didn't know what her reaction was going to be...so it was a shock. And then Ahmed arrived here so happy... So I thought, it's not for me to tell him anything... Hadeel should be the one to tell him... It's her marriage after all.

*(**HADEEL** is coughing.)*

BANA. What was Hadeel supposed to tell him?

YOUSSIF. About our conversation.

BANA. That you were in love with her?

YOUSSIF. Yes... No.

BANA. No?

YOUSSIF. Yes.

HADEEL. Youssif...

BANA. Yes or no?

(**YOUSSIF** *doesn't answer.*)

What was so confusing about your conversation?

(*No answer.*)

Tell him what?

AHMED. Yes. Tell me what?

HADEEL. Youssif...

BANA. What?

YOUSSIF. (*To* **HADEEL.**) You tell her.

HADEEL. Youssif...don't.

BANA. What?

YOUSSIF. (*To* **HADEEL.**) Tell her.

BANA. Tell me, Hadeel.

(*Pause.*)

What do you have to tell me, Hadeel?

HADEEL. That I'm in love with Youssif.

BANA. Ha.

AHMED. Hadeel.

HADEEL. Yes... I said that I'm in love with him.
(*To* **YOUSSIF.**) But I don't love you. I never loved you.
Never.

BANA. I don't understand.

HADEEL. Listen. When Youssif arrived here he said that he
loves me and that he wants to marry me.

BANA. (*To* **YOUSSIF.**) You proposed to her?

AHMED. But Hadeel...

HADEEL. Please. Please. Let me finish. Let me... He proposed.
And it was so hard... So hard. When you asked me

to marry you you broke three hearts, Youssif, your girlfriend's, your brother's, and mine. I didn't know what to do... I was... Ahmed was about to arrive and so were you, so I decided to lie. Yes. I lied. I told him that I loved him and that...that I would marry him... But it wasn't true. It wasn't. I was just desperate. I just wanted to be by myself for a few moments so I could...think. Just think. And I was so afraid. He wanted to touch me... And I didn't want to hurt anyone. I just wanted to protect all of you from...suffering.

BANA. But that's impossible. We are all here to suffer. Life is suffering.

HADEEL. I know.

AHMED. Well, not for me. I have been happy all my life. Until now...

HADEEL. Ahmed... I would never lie to you... Neither to you, Bana. I wasn't going to keep this a secret forever... (*To* **AHMED.**) I was going to tell you the truth. I would never live happily with a lie in my heart.

YOUSSIF. But you did lie to me.

HADEEL. No, I didn't.

YOUSSIF. You did.

HADEEL. For a little while, maybe, but...

BANA. It's all right, Hadeel. You did right. She did it for us, Ahmed.

HADEEL. Thank you, Bana. Now let's just forget it.

BANA. Yes. But before... I'm just really... My head is... I have just one doubt... It's just...

HADEEL. Let's watch TV.

>   (*They watch TV.*)
>
>   (*Pause.*)
>
>   (**BANA** *turns it off.*)

BANA. Wait.

>   (*Pause.*)

Forgive me. It's a doubt. You did tell him that you loved him?

HADEEL. What?

AHMED. Stop it Bana, it's over.

BANA. Please, Ahmed... Just let me. I need... Hadeel... How did you tell Youssif you loved him?

HADEEL. Bana...

BANA. Please tell me.

AHMED. Bana, please.

HADEEL. No, Ahmed... It's fine... I just said that I loved him.

BANA. How?

YOUSSIF. Bana...

BANA. Shut up. I need to see. Tell him again.

HADEEL. To him?

BANA. Yes. To his face.

HADEEL. OK. I just told him, *I love you.*

BANA. What else?

HADEEL. I said, I do. I do want to marry you.

BANA. What else?

AHMED. Stop it.

HADEEL. It's not fair.

BANA. Tell the truth, Hadeel. For once in your life tell the fucking truth.

HADEEL. Youssif, I'm so dirty. So, so dirty. You are so... you disgust me but...every time you and Bana come to watch TV...I want to scream TAKE ME with you, Youssif. TAKE ME WITH YOU. Drag me to your bed. I want to wash your hair. I want to see you smoke. I want to kiss your leather jacket. I want to see you eat and when you are done I want to lick your plate until it's completely clean.

BANA. Fuck.

AHMED. Hadeel.

HADEEL. I can't lie. I can't lie.

BANA. You truly love him, don't you?

HADEEL. Bana...

BANA. Do you love him?

HADEEL. I do. I love him with all my heart. I want him to sleep on top of me for the rest of my life. I love him as if he were a horse. And I tried to protect you, Bana. I tried to give him up in order to protect you but I can't live with a secret. I can't. And the two of you are the most wonderful people in the world but Youssif is my king. My new Caesar. He is my dinner. My swine. I'm so sorry... Everything is destroyed.

AHMED. It's over.

BANA. Thank you. Thank you, my friend. I was at the studio all day...working. I'm playing a woman who gets a heart transplant. Her name is May. And she falls in love with the husband of the woman who gave her her heart when she died. At one point he tells me, "You know... That heart has never been broken. I never stopped loving her." And I answer, "Then don't break it now. This heart is yours again. It's yours... Take it. But now it comes in this new body... Take your heart and take this weak, broken, beautiful body."

HADEEL. Please forgive me. Forgive me.

> *(She coughs. She walks to the table. Drinks water. She collapses and falls to the floor.)*
>
> *(The rest try to help her. She stays down.)*

BANA. Hadeel.

YOUSSIF. Hadeel.

AHMED. Love...

BANA. What's wrong?

YOUSSIF. Hadeel.

AHMED. Someone call an ambulance.

YOUSSIF. She doesn't have a pulse.

BANA. Hadeel. Sister...

YOUSSIF. She's dead.

AHMED. No.

YOUSSIF. She's dead.

>*(Pause.)*

AHMED. My love.

YOUSSIF. My Hadeel…

BANA. Shut up, Youssif.

YOUSSIF. I can't.

BANA. Shut up, Youssif. Shut up. Shut up. Shut. Up.

>*(They surround **HADEEL**. Slowly, **BANA** opens the window, almost jumps out.)*

>*(She takes a microphone and notes from the window. A spotlight comes up. She finds her light downstage as **LAURA**.)*

LAURA. *(To audience.)* Hello. I would like to say a couple of words… As you know the name of this play is Kiss. We discovered it not long ago, by chance, on the Internet when we were doing some research about the difficult situation for young writers in Syria during the current war…over there… We basically stumbled on this short play called Boosa, which means Kiss, originally, and we were immediately struck by its raw strength and the very interesting and indirect way in which it tries to convey the emotion of what it means and feels like to live in Damascus right now. We assume this happens in Damascus though it's not explicit in the text. So, soon after reading it we decided to stage it here, but it was really hard to secure the rights because of the language limitation and also, as much as we tried, we couldn't reach the author. The only thing we knew about her was that she was a young woman, that she had written the play in 2013, and that her name was *(Reads.)* Ameera…

ANDREA. Al Diri.

LAURA. Ameera Al Diri. Thank you. So we began rehearsing the play anyway hoping to be able to contact Ameera in the future during the rehearsal process. Well, now

I'm happy to say that finally, after several months of searching, just a few days ago, we received an email from a Syrian film director living in Turkey saying that he knew a Jordanian writer living in Cairo who actually knew Ameera and that she could be reached through a contact at the Red Cross in Lebanon. So finally, after a long time and with the help of a lot of people, they were able to contact her and arrange a call. Right now she's in Lebanon waiting to talk to us a little bit about her wonderful play so...you are all invited to stay. Please. Thank you.

> *(A screen appears on the stage.* **LAURA** *asks* **MARTIN** *to set up the connection.)*

And I'm sorry but I have to say I'm a little bit nervous because we haven't been able to talk to her or email her at all before this call. So... I'm sure the actors are nervous as well. And I'm sorry, I forgot to say that aside from being an actor I am also the director of this production. Yes. Sorry. Thank you. *(To* **MARTIN.***)* How are we doing there?

MARTIN. We're ready.

LAURA. Oh. OK. Then please go.

MARTIN. Oh. I was just waiting for you.

LAURA. I'm sorry. I thought you were...

MARTIN. No, sorry. My fault. My fault. Here...

> *(Skype connects.)*

LAURA. Oh... Here we go.

> *(The call is picked up. A young* **WOMAN** *appears on the screen in sunglasses and a blonde wig.)*

Hello.

> *(The* **WOMAN** *struggles to speak English and has a thick Arabic accent.)*

WOMAN. Hello.

LAURA. Hello... Can you hear us well?

WOMAN. Yes...

LAURA. Great. Thank you very, very much for this contact. It's really wonderful to have you here.

WOMAN. Thank you for having me.

LAURA. Great. Thank you. Let's start.

WOMAN. Of course.

> *(The **INTERPRETER** comes on the screen. She is a young white woman who works at an international NGO.)*

LAURA. Let me start by saying that we have just finished a performance of Boosa, which we translated as Kiss, and the audience is still here. And... Well, I'm the director and here are the other three actors because I also perform... Can you see them?

WOMAN. Yes. Hello.

ALL. Hello.

MARTIN. salaam alaikum.

WOMAN. alaikum salaam.

LAURA. Well. First congratulations.

WOMAN. I have a translator for the English.

LAURA. Thank you. Perfect. Hello. So can you tell us a little bit about yourself?

INTERPRETER. fi-ki ti'lilī-lna 3an-ik shway.

WOMAN. 3anni ana?

INTERPRETER. About me?

LAURA. Just a little bit.

WOMAN. harabt min ash-shām wa halla' sirt b-lubnān, ba3īde 3n ahlī. u-hōn ana 3ayshe...u-l-hilal il-aḥmar 3am yisā3id-ni... ana li-ḥālī.

INTERPRETER. Well... I escaped Damascus and right now I'm in Lebanon, separated from my family. I'm living here with the help...with the Red Crescent... I'm alone.

> *(Pause.)*

LAURA. Well... I hope you are well now.

WOMAN. Yes. Thank you.

(*Pause.*)

LAURA. Good. Great. I know that this play was written during the war.

WOMAN. eh na3m, inkatbet bi-shahr aylūl fi sint alfēn u klit-3ash u 'idirt ḥammil-ha lil-internet bi-tishrīn al-awwal.

INTERPRETER. Yes. It was written in September of 2013 and I was able to upload it to the Internet in October.

LAURA. Great. So...first I wanted to ask you what this play means in the context of the current war...

INTERPRETER. hay almasrahiyye shu b-ta3ni fi siyā' al-ḥarb al-ḥālīyye?

WOMAN. tayyib bi-sūrīa naḥnu mubdi3īn b-intāj al-musalsalāt. min-ḥibb-ha ktīr u-3adatan nitfaraj 3alayha ma3 al-ahl u-rif'āt-na u-nitsalla fī-ha u-mnākol akl ṭayyib ṭabakhnā-h khuṣūsi la-hēk munāsabāt.

INTERPRETER. In Syria we are very good at producing soap operas. We like them very much and we usually watch them with family and friends around wonderful food we cook especially for the occasion.

LAURA. So this play is supposed to be a kind of soap opera?

INTERPRETER. ya3ni-b-tu3tabir hay almasrahiyye musalsal?

WOMAN. ...b-3ata'id eh...bass mu tamāman...ma bi'dir ashraḥ-lik.

INTERPRETER. I guess so...but not exactly. I can't really explain it.

LAURA. Great. If it's all right the actors are going to be asking you some questions.

WOMAN. Yes, of course.

MARTIN. Thank you. I wanted to know if the play was ever produced in Damascus

INTERPRETER. in3arḍit hay almasrahiyye bish-shām min 'abl?

WOMAN. Yes.

MARTIN. Good. And… I don't know if you can see it but this stage creates the fiction of a – it's basically a television set. Can you see it?

INTERPRETER. ma ba3rif idha fīki tshūfi, bass hadha l-masraḥ b-yikhla' al-khayāl…3amaliyyan huwe 3ibara 3an 3amal estudio telefiziūni. fīki tshūfī-h?

WOMAN. la, mā fī-ni shūf shī.

INTERPRETER. No, I can't see anything.

MARTIN. Well… Is this idea in any way similar to the one you developed in Damascus?

WOMAN. ma 3am b-esma3. [I couldn't hear.]

INTERPRETER. Can you repeat that?

MARTIN. Because for us it was very important to convey the sense of intense love and heartbreak.

INTERPRETER. li-anno…kunna muhtammīn bi-shlōn min-3abbir 3an ash-shu3ūr bilḥubb il-3mī' u bil-ḥasra.

WOMAN. Yes.

LAURA. *(To* **MARTIN.***)* You have to repeat the same question.

MARTIN. Yes…

WOMAN. 'abl kull shī lāzim 'ul inno l-masraḥiyye kull-a khayāl. baladna indamarit, ḥayātna itḥaṭamit ' il-masraḥiyye 3am itḥāwal tikhla' faḍā' lil-ḥanīn u lil-nustaljiya.

INTERPRETER. I have to say that the play is above all a fantasy. Our country has been completely destroyed and our lives have been broken, so the play tries to create a space for nostalgia.

MARTIN. Nostalgia for the soap opera?

INTERPRETER. nustaljiya lil-musalsal?

WOMAN. Yes.

MARTIN. You miss soap operas?

WOMAN. eh bass lissa fīh 3ndna musalsalāt.

INTERPRETER. Yes. But soap operas still exist.

LAURA. Yes. Let's talk about something else.

WOMAN. ana mushtā'a lil-musalsalāt li-anni mushtā'a l-abkī, mushtā'a l-abkī was-sabab ashyā' ktīr basīṭa. almasraḥiyye 3am tikhla' 3ālam khayāli– fīh... al-mushkila alwaḥīde hiye alḥubb. ilna al-ḥubb wu-l-wijdān ṭarī'a li-t-tawāṣul ma3 hawiyit-na, t-tawāṣul ma3 māḍī-na, kamān ṭarī'a lil-ḥanīn ila l-waṭan al-maf'ūd.

INTERPRETER. I do miss soap operas because I miss crying for...simple things. The play creates a fictional world in which one of the only problems is just...love. And for us romantic love is a way of connecting with our identity, our past, and also longing for our lost country.

MARTIN. So in your production you created a fictional set of a fictional television melodrama?

INTERPRETER. idhan b-intāj-ik khala'ti sinārīu khayāli li-musalsal khayāli...mazbūṭ?

WOMAN. No.

MARTIN. Why not?

WOMAN. lianno hadha shī mustaḥīl halla'. ḥawādith almasraḥiyye kull-ha bi-oḍet al-'a3deh fi bēt 3ādi lianno hadōl al-amākin hinnen al-amākin al-waḥīde illi mni'dir mnkūn fī-ha. mā fī masraḥ shaghghāl u mā mniḥsin niṭla3 bil-lēl. al-masraḥiyye it'allafit li-oḍet al-'a3deh oḍet al-'a3deh al-ha'ī'īyye aw shu illi ba'yān min-a. bil-ha'ī'a intāj-na kān yu3raḍ li-nās ktīr 'alīle, ya3ni sha''a fīha ḥīṭān mabkhūshe min ākhir qaṣaf. bass mā 3andna ay khayār u ṭab3an kunna mnisma3 kamān ṣawt raṣāṣ.

INTERPRETER. Because that would be impossible right now. The play happens in the living room of a regular home because right now those are the only places available to us. There are no working theaters and we can't really go out at night. So the play was written for real living rooms or what's left of them. In fact our production was done for a few people in an apartment that had holes in the walls due to the recent bombing. But we had no choice. And of course there were real gunshots in the background.

LAURA. That's very interesting.

WOMAN. intū 3amiltu dhat ish-shī?

INTERPRETER. Did you do that?

LAURA. What?

WOMAN. ṣot ar-raṣāṣ?

INTERPRETER. The gunshots?

LAURA. No. Not exactly because we couldn't contact you before to learn all the details...

WOMAN. bass ar-raṣāṣ bi-n-naṣṣ.

INTERPRETER. But the gunshots were in the text.

LAURA. Yes...they were. But let's... I want to know... So beyond the aesthetics of the soap opera, let's leave that behind for a minute, the play is almost funny at times. Was that something you were looking for?

INTERPRETER. ghēr jamaliyyet al-musalsal, khallini itruk hadh ash-shi shway, al-masraḥiyye be-ḍaḥḥik aḥyānan. hadh illi intī kunti 3am te'ṣudi?

WOMAN. No.

LAURA. Great. Thank you.

DANIEL. May I?

LAURA. Of course.

DANIEL. Thank you. Hello. So... At one point my character...

LAURA. Who do you play?

DANIEL. Oh. Sorry. Sorry. I play Youssif. Sorry.

WOMAN. Yes.

DANIEL. I have a question about the character... It struck me as interesting that when Bana...

INTERPRETER. 3andi su'āl 3an ash-shakhṣiyye... fīh laḥza muthīra li-ihtimām lamma Bana...

LAURA. Played by me...

WOMAN. Yes.

DANIEL. Yes... When she arrives from work, she's an actress, she has been working on the television station or studio, and she arrives...and says that she has kissed someone...

INTERPRETER. ...eh... lamma btirja3 min ash-shughl, hiye mumaththile, rāḥit u istighilit bi estudiu u-btūṣal...u-bit'ūl inno bāsat ḥadda...

WOMAN. Yes.

DANIEL. Yes. But Youssif doesn't ask... He doesn't really know. But he's not really jealous, or at least he doesn't want to know who did she kiss. He just asks how. So I wonder...

INTERPRETER. ēh, bass yūsuf ma byis'al...huwa anijd ma bya3rif, bass huwe mū ghayrān aw 3ala l-a'all ma bidd-o ya3rif mīn bāsat, huwe bass 3mm yis'al kēf, fa batsā'al...

WOMAN. Yes?

(*Pause.*)

DANIEL. Did you hear the question?

WOMAN. Yes.

DANIEL. And what is the answer?

WOMAN. ṭayyib...izā kunt ṣūrī raḥ tefham inno Bana shakhṣiyye mustawḥāh min mumaththile mashhūra ktīr.

INTERPRETER. So...if you are from Syria you would understand that Bana is a...representation of a really famous actress.

LAURA. A real person?

WOMAN. eh, ism-hā Mayye Skaf, fi nihāyit al-masraḥiyye Bana bit'ūl inno bitmaththil shakhṣiyye ism-a Mayy.

INTERPRETER. Yes. Her name is May Skaf, in fact at the end Bana says that she is playing a character called May.

LAURA. Yes. A fictional character named May?

INTERPRETER. shakhṣiyye khayāliyye ism-a Mayy?

WOMAN. ēh bass Mayy Skaf al-ḥa'ī'iyye min ahamm al-nāshiṭīn illi ihtajū 3ala an-niẓām wa 3alanan bil-wa't al-ḥālī hiye min anshaṭ-un. khilāl mu3zam almasraḥiyye ma b-ta3rif mīn hiye Bana lākin lamma btūṣal mut-a'khkhire u-bit'ūl inno hiye mumaththile, al-wāhid byifham fawran inno mā bāsat ḥadda fi3liyyan u-inno ta'khīr-ha fil-wāqi3 bi-sabab i3tiqāl-ha min fer3 al-aman mitl Mayy Skaf al-ḥa'ī'īyye.

INTERPRETER. Yes. But the real May Skaf is one of the most visible and active fighters currently protesting publicly against the regime. So, during most of the play you don't really know who Bana is, but when she arrives late, and says that she's an actress, one immediately understands that she hasn't actually kissed anyone, but that in fact she's late because she has been detained by the police, just like the real May Skaf.

LAURA. Oh...

WOMAN. Yes.

DANIEL. But Youssif understands that May, sorry, that Bana has been detained?

INTERPRETER. bass Yūsuf byifham inno Bana akhadu-ha?

WOMAN. ēh, Bana ma 3am bit'ūl bi-shakl mubāshir bass bit'ūl inno bāsat ḥadda u hādha ya3ni iḍṭar-rat 3ala tajāwuz al-ḥadd,u inno kānat ḥamīmiyye ma3 ḥadda. bi-hay al-ḥāle hiya 3anīfe...kānat muwājaha 3nīfe.

INTERPRETER. Yes. Bana doesn't say it explicitly but she does say that she kissed someone, which means that she has been forced to cross a line, that she has been intimate with someone. In this case it's a violent encounter.

LAURA. And... When you say intimate...do you mean? ... Sorry, what do you mean?

WOMAN. mā bazunn inno Mayy Skaf ightasbit khilāl wa't-ha bil-mu3taqal, lamma stajwabū-hā.

INTERPRETER. I don't think May Skaf was raped during her time in prison, when she was interrogated.

LAURA. She was raped?

WOMAN. lā...al-ightiṣāb 3am byiṣīr wēn mā kān bi sūrīa.

INTERPRETER. Maybe. Probably... Rape is happening all over Syria.

LAURA. Yes.

MARTIN. Do you mean raped as a form of torture done by the police and the government forces?

INTERPRETER. 'aṣd-ik furū3 al-aman b-yisthikhdamu al-ightiṣāb ka-nō3 min at-ta3dhīb bil-mu3taqal?

   (Pause.)

WOMAN. befaḍḍil ma a'ūl.

INTERPRETER. I'd rather not say.

MARTIN. Why?

WOMAN. ma biddi 'ūl shī. [I don't want to say anything.]

INTERPRETER. She doesn't want to talk about it...

DANIEL. I'm sorry but just to be clear... The kiss means that Bana was raped by the police?

WOMAN. ana āsife. ma rah i'dir jāwib.

INTERPRETER. I am sorry. I can't answer.

LAURA. So she was raped?

ANDREA. You don't have to say it. We understand.

WOMAN. Thank you. minshān ḥēk lābse naḍḍarāt u-bārūke.

INTERPRETER. That's the reason I'm wearing glasses and a wig.

LAURA. So the word "kiss"... When she says she kissed someone, it doesn't mean she was unfaithful?

WOMAN. No.

LAURA. I see.

DANIEL. Thank you. I'm sorry if I...

MARTIN. May I?

DANIEL. Of course.

MARTIN. Hello.

ANDREA. *(To* **MARTIN.***)* Please don't...

MARTIN. *(To* **ANDREA.***)* Let's not... Let me.

ANDREA. OK.

MARTIN. I play Ahmed. So...towards the end Ahmed says, I don't believe in anyone anymore... So that always struck me as strange because, in general, why does the play have to end on such a sour note? For all I know we need to be able to see love win at the end. It's part of the melodramatic style, isn't it?

INTERPRETER. ana bel3ab dōr Ahmad.... bil-nihāye Ahmad byi'ūl: ma be-āmin bi-ayyi ḥadda ba3d halla'... hādh gharīb mu hēk? lēh lāzim tikhlaṣ almasraḥiyye bi-tarī'a hazīne hēk? bil melodrama, al-ḥubb ghālib bil-nihāye. mū hēk?

WOMAN. ...fahimt 3alek...bass bazunn...bin-nihāye al-ḥubb ghallāb...

INTERPRETER. I understand. But I guess that at the end love does win...

MARTIN. What do you mean?

WOMAN. sa3b 3alayyi aḥki 3an almasraḥiyye bi-hēk tafāṣīl bass khallī-ni 'ūl inno l-masrahiyye mū 3ibāra 3an al-shakhṣiyyāt nafs-ha, hiye 3ibāra 3an al-jumhūr illi byijtimi3 li-yitfaraj wa li-yiḥissu – li-mudde 'aṣīre ktir – bi-shi mukhtalif. bi-shi gher al-ḥarb. lianno al-ḥarb sa3be u-kull-na ṣirnā minshakkik bi-mawḍū3 al-ḥubb... kamān, khilāl al-ḥarb al-ḥubb ṣār a'wa wa aktar...ma ba3rif idha fahimt shu ba'ṣud?

INTERPRETER. It's hard for me to talk about the play in such detail, but let me say that the play is not about the characters themselves but about the audience who gathers around to see it and feel for a few minutes something else, something that is not war. But the war is hard and we all have become skeptics when it comes to love... And also...during war love becomes more intense. I don't know if I'm making sense.

MARTIN. Yes, you are!

LAURA. Could you tell us what's going on right now in Syria?

INTERPRETER. ma3 lēsh ti'līl-na shu illi 3am byiṣīr juwāt sūrīa halla'?

WOMAN. i'rū al-jarayid.

INTERPRETER. Everything is in the newspapers.

(Pause.)

WOMAN. al-hāwin 3am tinzil min al-sama. shu biddkun ta3rfū aktar min hēk?

INTERPRETER. Bombs are falling from the sky. What else do you need to know?

LAURA. Yes, thank you.

ANDREA. Thank you. I play Hadeel... So... We were really afraid... Well, when we were rehearsing the play we didn't know how the audience was going to react... Because to talk so openly and explicitly about feelings... it's hard to...

INTERPRETER. shukran. ana dōr Hadeel. kinna mnkhāf... lamma kinna 3am nitdarrib ma kinna mna3rif shu 3m byṣīr, shu rah ykūn raddit fi3l al-jumhūr.... alkalām al-ṣarīḥ 3an al-shu3ūr mū sahl...

DANIEL. Yes.

ANDREA. Can you help me?

DANIEL. Yes... Sure... I guess that when we talk about love... here. We are never so explicit. We don't, especially in America, in theatre, we don't say what we feel, because it may sound tasteless...or even ridiculous. We understand that cultures are different but this kind of melodrama sometimes is just pathetic and even ridiculous. Which is what makes it interesting. But we were afraid that the audience was going to laugh and just walk out of the theater.

LAURA. No... I don't think we all agree with that.

WOMAN. Hello?

LAURA. Yes...hello.

WOMAN. 'ana asif likunani lm 'asmae ma qalah alsyd lltw, hal yumkinuk 'an tueidah, min fadalk?

INTERPRETER. I'm sorry but I did not hear what the gentleman just said, could you repeat it, please?

LAURA. Yes, of course. I'll do it. We were saying that the final moment of the death of Hadeel is really interesting because she dies... And for us that moment is just the true height, the top of the melodramatic form, because she dies basically from a broken heart.

INTERPRETER. kunna 3am mn'ūl inno al-laḥza al-akhīre lamma betmūt Hadeel... hay al-laḥza muthīre lil-ihtimām li'anno hiye bitmūt... bi-n-nisba il-na hay al-laḥza hiye al-qimme al-ḥa'ī'īyye, qimmet taṣwīr al-meludrama, li'anno betmūt 3amaliyyan li'anno inkasar 'alb-a.

WOMAN. Yes.

LAURA. Did you hear?

WOMAN. Yes, I did.

ANDREA. Great. And I think that's beautiful too, because she dies out of the pain she feels after hurting her friend Bana so much.

INTERPRETER. 3azīm, bi-ra'yī hādha shi ḥilw kamān li'anno hiyye btmūt min al-'alam illi bthiss fīh ba3dma jarḥit rafī'it-ha Bana.

LAURA. Yes. She lies and takes away her boyfriend.

INTERPRETER. btikzib u btakhud ḥabīb-a.

ANDREA. Yes. So in a way the play is defending the idea of honesty and truth. And how lying to your own people can even kill you. And if you extrapolate that to the national level it becomes very political in the context of what's going on in Syria as a whole...

INTERPRETER. ēh, fa-izan al-masraḥiyye btit-'akkad fikrit al-ṣarāḥa u-l-ha'ī'a. kēf al-kizb 3ala sha3b-ak mumkin hatta yi'tul-ak. u-iza kabbar-na al-ṣūra lil-mustawā al-waṭanī, btṣīr al-ṣūra siya-siyye ktīr ma3 kull shi illi 3am byiṣīr fi sūrīa...bi-shakl 3āmm.

WOMAN. afwan, 'ālat innu mātit li'anno 'alb-a inkasar?

INTERPRETER. Excuse me? Did you say that she dies from a broken heart?

ANDREA. Yes. Before.

WOMAN. But she doesn't die of a broken heart.

(*The* **INTERPRETER** *is called away and leaves.*)

ANDREA. What?

WOMAN. She doesn't die of a broken heart.

ANDREA. You are saying she doesn't die of a broken heart?

WOMAN. No. She's coughing.

ANDREA. She's coughing?

LAURA. Yes.

ANDREA. What?

WOMAN. In the play there are several moments in which Hadeel is coughing.

ANDREA. Oh. Yes. There are several moments in which Hadeel is coughing...

LAURA. Yes, of course. She's coughing.

WOMAN. Did you do the coughing?

ANDREA. Yes, we did it.

LAURA. Yes, we did the coughing three times. It's in the text.

WOMAN. Great... So, as you know, the meaning of that recurring cough is that Hadeel has been exposed to chemical weapons.

   (Silence.)

The play is inspired by the chemical weapons attack in Damascus.

Hadeel has inhaled the gases and is not thinking well. That's why she lies to her lovers and changes her mind so absurdly. We basically see her losing her mind. And also...we see her dying.

LAURA. Sure. She lies to her lovers and loses her mind and dies because of the chemical gases.

WOMAN. That's the reason why at the end of the play the other characters don't really ask why she died. They know it because she's coughing.

ANDREA. Thank you.

WOMAN. Yes.

LAURA. So, it's not a melodrama after all?

WOMAN. Not really. She has been poisoned.

LAURA. No. She has been poisoned... Wow. This is so interesting. So...

   *(The **WOMAN** speaks to the **INTERPRETER**, who is outside the screen.)*

WOMAN. I'm sorry... I have to go.

LAURA. You have to go?

WOMAN. Yes... This office was... They tell me that I have to go.

LAURA. I'm sorry, but we wanted to give the audience the chance to ask some questions.

WOMAN. Maybe next time.

LAURA. But before you go, could you please give me your email so I can send you the video of tonight?

WOMAN. boosa2013@gmail.com.

LAURA. boosa2013@gmail.com... Thank you, Ameera... I'll write you tonight. Thank you very much.

WOMAN. Thank you... I'm sorry... What did you call me?

LAURA. What?

WOMAN. Did you say my name?

LAURA. Your name? Yes.

WOMAN. What did you call me?

LAURA. What we called you? Ameera...

WOMAN. Ameera?

LAURA. Yes, yes.

WOMAN. But I'm not Ameera.

LAURA. You are not Ameera?

WOMAN. No.

LAURA. You are not Ameera? And who are you?

WOMAN. I'm Ameera's sister.

LAURA. She...is your sister?

WOMAN. Yes.

LAURA. Oh, I'm sorry. This is great... Sorry. It's a big misunderstanding...

WOMAN. Yes.

LAURA. Can we talk to her?

> *(Pause.)*

Where is she?

WOMAN. She's dead.

LAURA. What?

WOMAN. She's dead.

LAURA. Dead?

WOMAN. Yes.

> *(Pause.)*

She died last November.

LAURA. Oh. I'm so sorry.

WOMAN. You thought I was Ameera?

LAURA. Yes.

WOMAN. I'm her sister.

LAURA. Her sister... Yes. I see. Sorry.

WOMAN. Yes.

LAURA. If I may... How did she die?

WOMAN. The government attacked our neighborhood in Damascus with bombs...and one of their bombs destroyed our apartment. And Ameera died.

LAURA. We are so very sorry.

ALL. Sorry.

WOMAN. Yes. A lot of people have died.

LAURA. What is your name?

WOMAN. I'd rather not say.

LAURA. Well... Thank you very, very much. It's... This talk has been really...helpful. And where are you now?

WOMAN. In a refugee camp. I have to go.

LAURA. Yes, of course. And I'll send you the video...

WOMAN. Thank you. Bye.

LAURA. Bye.

> *(Silence. Nobody moves. The actors gather and discuss. It's inaudible.)*

> *(**LAURA** walks downstage, speaks to the audience.)*

We'll start over.

> *(The play starts over in a heightened, more intense state. They try to get it right this time. The lights shift.)*

(**HADEEL** *coughs three times, then collapses.*)

YOUSSIF. Hello.

HADEEL. Hello.

YOUSSIF. Choose me, Hadeel...choose me. Forgive me for being so honest. I just want you to be my wife.

HADEEL. Youssif...

YOUSSIF. What?

HADEEL. Please.

YOUSSIF. Be my wife.

HADEEL. TAKE ME WITH YOU. I just want to kiss your leather jacket.

YOUSSIF. Please marry me.

HADEEL. Don't touch me. Not now. If we start we won't be able to stop.

AHMED. Listen... I'm going to marry her.

YOUSSIF. Who?

AHMED. Hadeel.

YOUSSIF. Hadeel?

AHMED. Of course.

YOUSSIF. Great. Congratulations. But don't ask her right now.

AHMED. Why?

YOUSSIF. It's not really romantic.

AHMED. I know. I don't care. I'm not romantic.

YOUSSIF. He is going to propose.

HADEEL. What?

YOUSSIF. He just told me. He is going to propose.

HADEEL. No... Why?

YOUSSIF. He is in love with you.

AHMED. Hello.

HADEEL. Hello.

YOUSSIF. Bye. Good luck.

AHMED & HADEEL. Thank you.

AHMED. Listen... Hadeel, we need to talk.

HADEEL. Yes.

AHMED. Hadeel, I want to give you my life. You are my life... I don't know, Hadeel. Will you marry me?

HADEEL. Ahmed... This is a surprise.

AHMED. I know.

HADEEL. So yes. I will marry you. Of course! Ahmed, my love! I'm so incredibly happy.

AHMED. We are getting married.

YOUSSIF. Yes?

AHMED. Yes.

YOUSSIF. Yes... Congratulations. Congratulations. You're going to be so happy.

HADEEL. Yes. But we are happy right now.

YOUSSIF. I would like to marry the woman I love.

HADEEL. Maybe you shouldn't propose tonight.

YOUSSIF. Why not?

BANA. Hi.

YOUSSIF. What's wrong?

BANA. I kissed someone.

YOUSSIF. What?

BANA. A kiss.

YOUSSIF. Bana...

BANA. What do you care so much? You weren't so upset when you were dumping me last night.

YOUSSIF. Did you kiss someone?

BANA. I did.

(Pause.)

HADEEL. Bana... Sit. I can't see you suffer like this. Listen. Youssif arrived early today...and he said that he loved me.

BANA. When?

HADEEL. Today.

AHMED. Today?

YOUSSIF. Everything is broken. This is total destruction. I can't even think.

HADEEL. I'm going to get married.

AHMED. Yes, but this, what happened here, changes everything.

BANA. Please, Ahmed. Don't do that. Don't. She loves you with all her heart and you know it.

YOUSSIF. Bana, please. You don't understand. I told Hadeel I love her. That much is true. And I am terribly terribly sorry.

BANA. What do you have to tell me, Hadeel?

HADEEL. Listen. When Youssif arrived here, he said that he loved me and that he wanted to marry me.

BANA. *(To* **YOUSSIF**.*)* You proposed to her?

AHMED. But Hadeel...

HADEEL. Please. I just wanted to protect all of you from suffering.

BANA. But that's impossible. Life is suffering.

HADEEL. I know.

AHMED. I have been happy all my life. Until now...

HADEEL. Let's watch TV.

BANA. Wait.

(Pause.)

Forgive me. It's a doubt. You did tell him that you love him?

HADEEL. What?

AHMED. Stop it, Bana, it's over.

BANA. Please, Ahmed... Just let me. I need... Hadeel... How did you tell Youssif that you love him?

HADEEL. Bana...

BANA. Please tell me.

AHMED. Bana, please.

HADEEL. No, Ahmed... It's fine... I just said that I loved him.

BANA. How?

YOUSSIF. Bana...

BANA. Shut up. I need to see it. Tell him again.

HADEEL. To him?

BANA. Yes. To his face.

HADEEL. OK. I just told him, *I love you.*

BANA. What else?

HADEEL. I said, I do. I do want to marry you.

BANA. What else?

AHMED. Stop it.

HADEEL. It's not fair.

BANA. Tell the truth, Hadeel. For once in your life tell the fucking truth.

HADEEL. Youssif, I'm so dirty. So, so dirty. You are so… you disgust me but…every time you and Bana come to watch TV…I want to scream TAKE ME with you, Youssif. TAKE ME WITH YOU. Drag me to your bed. I want to wash your hair. I want to see you smoke. I want to kiss your leather jacket. I want to see you eat and when you are done I want to lick your plate until it's completely clean.

BANA. Fuck.

AHMED. Hadeel.

HADEEL. I can't lie. I can't lie.

BANA. You truly love him, don't you?

HADEEL. Bana…

BANA. Do you love him?

HADEEL. I do. I love him with all my heart. I want him to sleep on top of me for the rest of my life. I love him like a horse. And I tried to protect you, Bana. I tried to give him up in order to protect you but I can't live with a secret. I can't. And the two of you are the most wonderful people in the world but Youssif is my king. My new Caesar. He is my dinner. My swine. I'm so sorry… Everything is destroyed.

AHMED. It's over.

BANA. Thank you. Thank you, my friend. I was at the studio all day…working. I'm playing a woman who gets a heart transplant. Her name is May. And she falls in love with the husband of the woman who gave her her heart when she died. At one point he tells me, "You know… That heart has never been broken. I never stopped loving her." And I answer, "Then don't break it now. This heart is yours again. It's yours… Take it. But now it comes in this new body… Take your heart and take this weak, broken, beautiful body."

> (**HADEEL** *coughs. She walks to the table, then collapses and falls to the floor.*)
>
> (*The others try to help her.*)

Hadeel.

YOUSSIF. Hadeel.

AHMED. Love…

BANA. What's wrong?

YOUSSIF. Hadeel.

She doesn't have a pulse.

BANA. Hadeel. Sister…

YOUSSIF. She's dead.

AHMED. No.

YOUSSIF. She's dead.

AHMED. My love.

YOUSSIF. My Hadeel…

BANA. Shut up, Youssif.

YOUSSIF. I can't.

BANA. Shut up, Youssif. Shut up. Shut up. Shut. Up.

> (*Pause. The actors circle up and talk inaudibly again.* **LAURA** *comes down to the audience.*)

LAURA. We'll keep going.

> (*The actors move at breakneck speed. Time warps. Lights shift.*)

(**HADEEL** *wakes up. She stands up.*)

HADEEL. I'm sorry.

AHMED. Are you OK?

YOUSSIF. What happened?

HADEEL. I don't know. It seems that I just died for a second...

BANA. Yes... Sit.

HADEEL. Thanks.

(*She sits.*)

BANA. Hadeel... Do you remember what just happened here?

HADEEL. I do.

BANA. Good. Hadeel...

YOUSSIF. Bana, stop.

AHMED. Bana. You're going to make her sick again.

BANA. Let me. It's important.

HADEEL. What?

BANA. Hadeel... You said you were in love with Youssif.

HADEEL. Yes. I did.

BANA. You said he was your swine.

HADEEL. Yes.

YOUSSIF. Bana...

BANA. I understand... I understand. Things like this happen every day.

HADEEL. What?

BANA. I forgive you, Hadeel. I forgive you. And I know we might never watch the soap opera again. We might not see each other again, but I just want to say that love is a wonderful thing. Love is a miracle. And when it happens we, as humans, we have to let it live, even if it kills us.

(**AHMED** *coughs.*)

YOUSSIF. Agh... Please... Bana.

HADEEL. Bana...

BANA. I'm sorry. That's all. I just want you to be happy.

HADEEL. Bana… You are an angel.

BANA. Yes. I guess I am.

YOUSSIF. Let's go, Hadeel.

AHMED. No.

YOUSSIF. Let's go.

AHMED. You can't leave me like this, Hadeel. Five minutes ago you were going to marry me.

HADEEL. I know. I'm sorry. But I have to go…

AHMED. Shit.

BANA. *(Breaks character, to* **HADEEL.***)* Keep going.

> *(Before leaving,* **HADEEL** *stops.)*

HADEEL. Before I leave, Ahmed… Can you look at me for a second.

AHMED. I can't.

HADEEL. Just look at me. I want to say good bye. Please.

> *(***AHMED** *looks at her.)*

Thank you… It's strange, isn't it?

AHMED. It is.

YOUSSIF. Let's go, Hadeel.

> *(***BANA** *coughs.)*

HADEEL. This is so strange. Your eyes…

AHMED. What?

BANA. Just go, Hadeel.

HADEEL. And not just your eyes. You're letting me go with Youssif…like it's nothing.

AHMED. Yes, because you're in love with him…

HADEEL. Yes. And Bana… She forgave me. She forgave me so…fast.

> *(***YOUSSIF** *coughs.)*

BANA. What?

HADEEL. You forgave me. Immediately.

BANA. What do you want, Hadeel?

HADEEL. I want to leave.

AHMED. Good.

BANA. Then leave.

HADEEL. Yes. But before I go...please answer... Did you sleep with Ahmed?

BANA. What?

AHMED. Hadeel...

HADEEL. Did you sleep with Ahmed?

BANA. Shut up, Hadeel.

HADEEL. Did you sleep with Ahmed? I just want to know.

AHMED. Stop it, Hadeel. You are crazy. You are crazy and I will not let you do any more harm to any of us.

YOUSSIF. *(To* **AHMED.***)* Shut the fuck up. She's just asking a simple question.

HADEEL. *(To* **YOUSSIF.***)* Don't talk to him like that.

YOUSSIF. *(To* **AHMED.***)* Who the fuck are you calling crazy? Five minutes ago you were going to marry her. Is she crazy because she doesn't love you anymore? Is she crazy for loving me? What does it matter? Just accept it. Life is suffering.

BANA. It's true.

HADEEL. What is true? *(Coughs.)*

BANA. I forgave you too...fast.

AHMED. Bana...

HADEEL. Why?

BANA. I forgave you because...

AHMED. *(Breaks character, to* **BANA.***)* Keep going.

BANA. Maybe you are right. There is something strange in Ahmed's eyes. And in mine too. They look dead, like dog eyes. And I think that is because I did sleep with Ahmed.

HADEEL. What?

YOUSSIF. Fuck.

HADEEL. You did?

BANA. Yes. We did. On this same sofa. You were away... We were watching a soap opera and...

HADEEL. What?

BANA. …It happened.

YOUSSIF. What happened?

BANA. I can't tell you. *(Coughs.)*

YOUSSIF. Of course you can't. It's just too beautiful, right? So beautiful that you had to keep it a secret. I know how it is. I know everything about loving secretly. I'm sure that this beautiful thing between you two happened many times, on this same couch. You don't have to tell me. First you feel something here and then you let yourself fall. You fall into the sea of love. And it's so beautiful that you have to put it into words, to make sure it's real. So while you are on the couch, doing it, you talk. You talk into each other's ear. Or even scream. You scream that you love each other. You scream each other's name. You scream that you have wanted this since the first time I saw you. And when it's over you hold each other and cry. You cry out of joy. You cry out of regret. You hate yourselves. You sit up on the couch and swear to each other that you will keep the secret forever. It happens every day.

HADEEL. Ahmed, I never let Youssif touch me.

AHMED. Please, don't even say that. You don't have the right to judge me right now. *(Coughs.)*

HADEEL. But he didn't touch me.

AHMED. But you thought about touching him. You had to fight the need to touch him. You thought about sleeping with him on that couch. You imagined him naked. You wanted to lick his leather jacket. You wanted to lick his bed, his spoon, his money. You said he was your elephant, your king, your swine. You said it, Hadeel.

HADEEL. I'm so glad we are breaking up, Ahmed. I'm so glad I didn't get pregnant.

AHMED. Me too.

YOUSSIF. Yes. Me too.

> *(Pause. **BANA** coughs.)*

YOUSSIF. Bana?

> *(Pause.)*

Bana...

AHMED. Bana.

> **(BANA** *coughs.)*

YOUSSIF. *(Breaks character, to* **BANA.***)* Keep going.

BANA. Life's not easy. I might be pregnant.

HADEEL. You might?

BANA. No. I *am* pregnant.

AHMED. Fuck.

> **(BANA** *laughs.)*

YOUSSIF. But Bana... Since when?

BANA. A couple of weeks.

HADEEL. Fuck.

YOUSSIF. Bana... This... This is something you have to tell. To tell *me*...

BANA. I know.

YOUSSIF. Bana...

HADEEL. I know what happens now.

YOUSSIF. *(Coughs.)* Hadeel...don't be... I'm sorry. Don't... just give me a minute here.

HADEEL. But someone has to smile. *(Coughs.)* And it can't be me. I'm losing you.

BANA. It should be me. I should be smiling.

YOUSSIF. I'm smiling.

> *(Pause.)*

AHMED. Then why don't you smile?

YOUSSIF. I am smiling.

AHMED. I'm not talking to you. Why are you not smiling, Bana?

BANA. Well... You know.

AHMED. Yes. I do. Now I know. *(Coughs.)*

(*Pause.*)

HADEEL. What do you know, Ahmed?

AHMED. Nothing.

HADEEL. What do you know, Ahmed?

YOUSSIF. What are you talking about?

BANA. I... The soap opera started a long time ago. We are missing the soap opera.

YOUSSIF. What are you talking about, Bana?

HADEEL. Don't you understand, Youssif?

YOUSSIF. Understand what? (*Coughs.*)

HADEEL. Tell him, Bana.

YOUSSIF. Tell me what?

(*Pause.*)

BANA. The baby might be Ahmed's.

YOUSSIF. Ahmed?

BANA. I'm sorry.

YOUSSIF. What?

BANA. Yes.

YOUSSIF. So it didn't happen long ago?

HADEEL. No. It happened just weeks ago. It might have happened this morning.

YOUSSIF. (*Loud.*) Fucking Assad.

HADEEL. Youssif.

YOUSSIF. (*To* **AHMED**.) Are you smiling right now?

AHMED. Yes. I am.

BANA. But a lot of people have kissed me.

HADEEL. Everyone wants to kiss you.

YOUSSIF. (*To* **AHMED**.) Did you hear that?

AHMED. Yes. I did. It might not be my baby after all.

YOUSSIF. (*Loud.*) Fucking Putin.

HADEEL. It could be anyone. Someone might knock the door right now and say, *I am the father*.

(*Pause.*)

BANA. We used to be a family.

HADEEL. We watched soap operas together.

AHMED. Yes. We ate. And smoked. And sang.

YOUSSIF. We loved two people at the same time.

BANA. What happened to us?

AHMED. We loved too much.

HADEEL. Don't give me that love bullshit again. This is not love. This is lust. You say you love but you behave like a horse. This is exactly the reason why I don't read the newspapers.

>　　　(*The actors sit on the couch and chairs, defeated.*)
>
>　　　(**BANA** *picks up the microphone.*)
>
>　　　(*The* **WOMAN** *from Skype,* **AMEERA'S SISTER**, *comes onstage and sits on the couch. She starts to sing "Yama Mweil El-Hawa?" ["Mother, What's With the Wind?"] quietly. The actors don't acknowledge her.*)

BANA. (*Speaks into the microphone, to the audience.*) Did you hear that? It sounds like fireworks. I don't know but today, when I was walking, everything seemed a little bit more empty. I feel like there's more...space. Or maybe less people. There used to be more. Maybe they stayed at home watching TV. Or maybe they are just... away. By the sea. But I'm sure they'll be back. They have to. There is a hole in the street and someone might fall into it. I think someone needs to fix that.

And they need to paint. The walls are...the color is not right. It's black. There is a lot of black. Black patches. Someone needs to paint those white. And I need a doctor, for my baby. And I need a school. But the school is empty. There are no children. Someone needs to teach them how to read. They need to learn how to cut paper with scissors. Those little paper dolls holding each other's hands. Holding hands like this family. And someone needs to teach them how to sing.

(*Pause.*)

(*Refers to* **AMEERA'S SISTER**.) One line from this song means: I would rather be stabbed than live under the rule of this bastard.

(**AMEERA'S SISTER** *sings the song as the lights fade, eventually singing in the dark.*)

End of Play

"YAMA MWEIL EL-HAWA?"
["MOTHER, WHAT'S WITH THE WIND?"]

Transliteration:

YAMMA, MWEYL EL HAWA, YAMMA, MWEYL-EYA
DARB EL KHANAJER WALA, HOKM EL-NATHEL FIYYA

W-MSHEET, TAHT E-SHITA, W-SHITA RAWWANI
W-SAIF LAMMA ATA, WALLA' MIN NEERANI
BIDAL 'OMRI ENFADA, NIDR LIL HURREYYA

YAMMA, MWEYL EL HAWA, YAMMA, MWEYL-EYA
DARB EL KHANAJER WALA, HOKM EL-NATHEL FIYYA

YA LEIL, SAH EL NADA, YESH-HAD 'ALA JRAHI
W-INSAL, JAISH EL 'AIDA, MIN KUL IL NAWAHI
WEL LEIL, SHEL EL RADA, 'AM YAT'ALLEM FIYYA

YAMMA, MWEYL EL HAWA, YAMMA, MWEYL-EYA
DARB EL KHANAJER WALA, HOKM EL-NATHEL FIYYA

BAROODEH FIL JABAL, A'LA MIN EL 'ALI
MEFTAH DARB IL AMAL, WEL AMAL FI RJALI
YASHA' BINA YA BATAL, AFDIK B'EENAYA

YAMMA, MWEYL EL HAWA, YAMMA, MWEYL-EYA
DARB EL KHANAJER WALA, HOKM EL-NATHEL FIYYA

Translation:

MOTHER WHAT'S WITH THE WIND?
MOTHER WHAT DOES IT WANT FROM ME?
I'D RATHER BE STABBED BY DAGGERS
THAN HAVE A BASTARD [SNAKE/UNJUST PERSON] RULE
    OVER ME

AND I WALKED BENEATH THE RAIN,
AND IT QUENCHED ME
AND WHEN THE SUMMER CAME BY
IT BURNED UP FROM MY FLAME
FOR AS LONG AS I LIVE
MY LIFE IS DEVOTED TO FREEDOM

MOTHER WHAT'S WITH THE WIND?
MOTHER WHAT DOES IT WANT FROM ME?

I'D RATHER BE STABBED BY DAGGERS
THAN HAVE A BASTARD [SNAKE/UNJUST PERSON] RULE
    OVER ME

"OH NIGHT," THE DEW DROPS CRIED OUT
TESTIFYING FOR MY WOUNDS
AND THE ARMY OF THE ENEMY CREPT FROM EVERY
    CORNER
AND THE NIGHT HAS SEEN DEATH
PRACTICING ITS TRADE ON ME

MOTHER WHAT'S WITH THE WIND?
MOTHER WHAT DOES IT WANT FROM ME?
I'D RATHER BE STABBED BY DAGGERS
THAN HAVE A BASTARD [SNAKE/UNJUST PERSON] RULE
    OVER ME

A RIFLE IN THE MOUNTAIN
HIGHER THAN HIGH
THE KEY TO THE PATH OF HOPE
MY PEOPLE ALL HEROES
I WOULD SACRIFICE MY EYES FOR YOU

MOTHER WHAT'S WITH THE WIND?
MOTHER WHAT DOES IT WANT FROM ME?
I'D RATHER BE STABBED BY DAGGERS
THAN HAVE A BASTARD [SNAKE/UNJUST PERSON] RULE
    OVER ME

مويليا يما الهوا مويل يما
فيا النذل حكم ولا الخناجر ضرب
رواني والشتا الشتا تحت ومشيت
نيراني من ولع أتى لما والصيف
للحرية ندر انفدى عمري بيضل
الهوا مويل يما
جراحي على يشهد الندى صاح ليل يا
النواحي كل من العدا جيش وانسل
بيا يتعلم عم الردى شاف والليل
العالي من أعلى الجبل بارودة الهوا مويل يما
برجالي والأمل الأمل درب مفتاح
بعينيا أفديك بطل يا شعبنا يا
الهوا مويل يما

Yama Mweil El-Hawa?

(Mother, What's With the Wind?)

Slowly

Traditional Arabic Song

11 VERSE 2
ya_leil,_ sah el_ na - da,_ yesh-had'a - la jra - hi_
13
w-in-sal,_ jai-sh-el'ai - da,_ min kul il na-wa - hi_
15
wel leil,_ shel_ el_ ra - da,_
16 D.C.
'am ya - t'al - lem_ fiy - ya
17 VERSE 3
ba - roo - deh fil ja - bal,_ a -'la min el 'a - li_
19
meft-ah_ darb il_ a - mal,_ wel a-mal fi rja - li_
21
ya - sha'_ bi - na_ ya_ ba - tal,_
22 D.C. al Fine
af - dik_ b'e - e - na - ya

www.ingramcontent.com/pod-product-compliance
Lightning Source LLC
Chambersburg PA
CBHW070400120726
47909CB00008B/2927